Tritely Challenged

Volume 2

Copyright © 2020 Christopher Fielden. All rights reserved.

The copyright of each story published in this anthology remains with the author.

Cover copyright © 2020 David Fielden. All rights reserved.

Chris's Colossal Cliché Count Writing Challenge was launched in conjunction with the inaugural Flash Fiction Festival.

First published June 2020.

The rights of the writers of the short stories published in this anthology to be identified as the authors of their work has been asserted in accordance with the Copyright, Designs and Patents Act 1988.

All rights reserved. No part of this publication may be reproduced, stored in a retrieval system, or transmitted in any form by any means, electronic, mechanical, photocopying, recording or otherwise, without the prior permission of the publishers.

You can learn more about Chris's Colossal Cliché Count Writing Challenge and many other writing challenges at:

www.christopherfielden.com

All characters in this publication are fictitious and any resemblance to real persons, living or dead, is purely coincidental.

ISBN: 9798646104053

DEDICATION

For all the keyworkers around the world who behaved so courageously during the COVID-19 pandemic.

TRITELY CHALLENGED

Chris Writefear, explaining the concept of cliché overuse to the legend that is Joody Higgins

INTRODUCTION 1

by Jude Higgins

It's an honour to write the introduction to the second volume of tritely challenged fictions. Writing with the intention of making common mistakes is such a great way to help stories flow on to the page. And clichés are very fun to deliberately insert into a piece. Thank you to Christopher Fielden for beginning the cliché challenge at the first ever Flash Fiction Festival in 2017. It's wonderful to see that the challenges are going strong three years later and continuing to raise money for charity.

Writers in this anthology have packed dozens of common phrases into their stories. There are many in the English language, and I expect in other languages too.

A quick glance through the tiny tales and you will find all categories of cliché. Here are a few:

- Body clichés: legs like jelly, stomach in knots, floods of tears, head over heels in love, like pulling teeth, gut-wrenching, gnarled hands
- Clichés concerning time: a split second, a blast from the past, faster than the speed of light
- Clichéd sayings: 'two wrongs don't make a right', 'actions speak louder than words', 'a chain is only as strong as the weakest link'

It would be quite something to do a count of all the clichés writers have used in the book and to note the ones that come up most frequently. We all have our favourites and are often cliché-blind – not even noticing how they creep on to the page when we attempt not to use them.

Apart from clichéd sentences, stories often have clichéd plots or characters. In competitions, a plot I've read over and over is when an aggrieved wife (it's usually a wife or girlfriend) plans a dastardly way of murdering her husband or lover. Poison is a favourite. Story titles can be clichéd too. 'Metamorphosis' is one often used.

The cliché-ridden stories in this volume will make you chuckle or laugh out loud because the language is so exaggerated. And having a laugh is the best way to learn anything.

I am sure you will enjoy the read.

Jude Higgins,
Writer, tutor & director of Flash Fiction Festivals, UK
May 2020
www.judehiggins.com

INTRODUCTION 2

by Chris Fielden

Welcome to the second cliché challenge anthology.

As Jude mentioned in her introduction, Chris's Colossal Cliché Count Writing Challenge was launched in June 2017 in conjunction with the UK's first ever festival dedicated to flash fiction.

Rest assured, as certain as the sun will rise and as sure as eggs are eggs, many writers overuse clichés from time to time. (How many clichés can you spot in the previous sentence? Too many… ☺.) The cliché challenge was launched to highlight this common mistake, give writers the experience of being published, support an amazing charity and to have fun with words.

The first anthology, *Tritely Challenged Volume 1*, was published in April 2018 and contained the first 100 stories submitted to the challenge.

Many of the stories in that book were written at the inaugural Flash Fiction Festival, by attendees. Since then, the challenge has remained popular with my website users, hence this book exists.

Tritely Challenged Volume 2 will be the last anthology published via the cliché writing challenge. It was a tough decision to make, but due to the number of challenges I run and the amount of time it takes to edit and publish these books, unfortunately producing multiple anthologies via every challenge is no longer viable. Therefore, I'm scaling things back.

I will be making similar changes to some of the other writing challenges over time to help maintain a manageable workload.

That said, the cliché challenge is still open and future

submissions will be published on my website. And book production won't stop all together. We will still publish some anthologies via the writing challenges, just not as many.

The stories in this book are presented in the order they were received. Each writer's biography appears with their story. Because this is the second clichéd collection, numbering starts at 101. Numbers 1 to 100 can be found within the pages of *Tritely Challenged Volume 1*.

The writers that have contributed to this cliché crammed tome have been inventive, entertaining and fervently overzealous in their cliché usage.

I hope you enjoy reading their tales as much as Jude and I have enjoyed presenting them.

Over and out.

Chris Fielden, Portishead, May 2020

INTRODUCTION 3

by Book Aid International

Around the world, millions of people live in a world with few books, or even no books at all. They cannot afford to buy books at home and in schools pupils must share just a few old textbooks. Libraries often offer the best opportunity for people to read, but even libraries often have just a few out of date books. This lack of books leaves children less able to succeed in school, prevents adults from learning throughout their lives and denies people the simple joy of reading.

At Book Aid International we believe that everyone should have access to books that will enrich, improve and change their lives. Every year, we send around one million brand new books to libraries, schools, universities, hospitals, refugee camps and prisons where people would otherwise have few opportunities to access books and read. In an average year, these books are read by an estimated 25 million people.

It costs just £2 to send another book, so every penny raised really makes a difference. We would like to thank the contributors and editors of this anthology for their support.

www.bookaid.org

ACKNOWLEDGMENTS

Big thanks to Flash Fiction Festival Director, Jude Higgins, and all the other festival organisers for helping me unleash the Cliché Challenge upon the planet. You can learn more about the festival here: www.flashfictionfestival.com

Thanks to David Fielden for designing the cover of this book and building and maintaining my website. Without him, I'd never have created a platform that allowed the writing challenges I run to be so successful. You can learn more about Dave's website building skills at: www.bluetree.co.uk

Finally, a tritely-worded big as a house (by and large) thank you to everyone who has submitted stories, supported this crazy idea and, in turn, Book Aid International. Without the support of all the writers who submit their stories, this simply wouldn't be possible.

TRITELY CHALLENGED

101: THE PUNDIT TREE

by Allen Ashley

"United were disgraceful. A bunch of pouting prima-donnas. They played like a load of strangers, Lee."

"That's true, Roy. City were shambolic. Keystone Cops defending. No organisation in midfield: four men all watching the ball; you could have thrown a blanket over them. No one prepared to put a shift in."

"And Gilbertini got an early bath when he made his mark on Andy Hopkins."

"Plenty of claret."

"He's got his arm out for leverage. Sure, his elbow smashes the guy's nose, but football's a contact sport. Too many namby-pambies throwing themselves over, trying to con the referee."

"All we want is consistency, Roy. Still, Lucescu was marginally offside for the goal."

"Nothing marginal. You're either onside, Lee, or you're off."

"At least it picked up in the second period. The first 45 minutes was a snooze fest."

"It was the classic game of two halves, Lee."

"It always is, Roy."

~

Allen Ashley's Biography

Allen Ashley is co-originator of the Sensory Challenge. His most recent book is the poetry collection *Echoes from an Expired Earth* (Demain Publishing, UK, 2020). He is President Elect of the British Fantasy Society.
　　www.allenashley.com

102: FIONA'S REFUSAL

by Lesley Anne Truchet

"When I met you it was love at first sight. I fell head over heels." Edward attempted to move his right hand higher.

"Weel they dae say love is blind." Fiona clamped the inquisitive fingers.

"Busy hands are happy hands," Edward leered.

"Aam nae in th'muid, dinna think you're gonnae hide th'salami, ye willna be caught with ye keks doon this afternoon."

"But my heart, you're drop dead gorgeous and a thing of beauty is a joy forever."

"Empty flattery willnae gie ye whit ye want."

"Fiona, you're putting a fly in the ointment, I'm dead serious."

"I'm nae bowled ower by yer words, Edward."

"What about these words? Will you marry me?"

"No."

"No?"

"Nay, Edward, Ah couldnae marry ye tae save mah life. Ye gab tae much in clichés."

~

Lesley Anne Truchet's Biography

Lesley Truchet has been writing for several years and has a number of short stories, articles and poetry published on paper and on the internet. She is currently writing her first novel.

103: PARADE

by Michael Rumsey

Against all the odds, the invitation came out of the blue.

Would some of us army veterans, now long in the tooth, be prepared to stand on ceremony shoulder to shoulder?

Of course, we were only too happy to take the plunge. It would be like being back in the saddle and we were assured of the red carpet treatment.

It was a case of best foot forward, spit and polish, get the lead out and, mark my words, no beating about the bush.

Several international veterans, some as tough as nails, had a vested interest. But to set the record straight and, in the long and short of it, not that it would be the end of the world and not due to a twist of fate, no Welshmen would take part. It's just that old Dai's never soldier.

~

Michael Rumsey's Biography

Michael has an ace up his sleeve in that he feels it is his rite to write trite, right? Therefore he does not want to be left out in the cold.

www.facebook.com/mrumsey

104: MOSEY

by Gavin Biddlecombe

Hank drew at Champion's reigns, directing him to the boisterous saloon, dismounted and moseyed up to the swinging doors, spurs clinking with each step.

The din settled within as the punters paused to examine their newest guest, silhouetted at the entrance. Hank ignored the rank, stale smell of sweat as he stepped forward, motioning to the barman.

"A bottle of sarsaparilla," he called.

The barman reached under the counter.

Hank gripped the handle of his Colt revolver.

The crowd held their breath.

The barman's hand appeared with a dirty brown bottle, which he then slid across towards Hank. He released his grip and reached for the bottle. A slight nod put the barman at ease.

A spittoon rang in the background as the folk began to settle, prompting the piano's jovial melody to pick up where it had been interrupted.

~

Gavin Biddlecombe's Biography

Gavin lives in Gibraltar with his wife and crazy little dog where he spends his free time reading, writing short stories and working on his photography. His focus at the moment is on short stories and flash fiction.

www.gavinbiddlecombe.wordpress.com

105: CAN I BE FRANK?

by David Silver

If the truth be known, I'm no great shakes with women. On the other hand, my pal Frank is a charmer. His signature chat-up line works its magic every time.

Frank makes a beeline for a pretty young thing and whispers into her shell-like, "There must be a thief in your family, because someone stole the stars and put them in your eyes."

One evening, I saw my dream woman across a crowded bar. Frank said, "Here's your chance. You must grasp the nettle when opportunity knocks."

I approached her, my legs like jelly, my stomach in knots, and mumbled, "Is there a thief in your family?"

The object of my affection burst into floods of tears. "I swear my brother is innocent. He was framed."

Frank took my arm in a vice-like grip and pulled me away. "Better luck next time. Now, let's get outta here."

~

David Silver's Biography

David Silver was a reporter, sub-editor and columnist on various newspapers in Greater Manchester, England. He retired in 2002 and from 2011-2016 wrote a column for *The Courier*, a weekly newspaper for UK expatriates in Spain.

106: MR GREEN FINGERS

by Len Saculla

Even as a city dweller, I wanted to have my own little acre. Sow some seeds, put down roots, see the green shoots appearing.

So now everything's coming up roses. Grow your own, they say. Dig for victory. Make hay while the sun shines.

Into every life a little rain must fall. Pennies from heaven for us green-fingered growers.

Anyhow, for hay you need grass. I'm not growing that here. Mainly because it's always greener on the other side.

The other side, eh? Where you go when you're pushing up the daisies.

Blooming weeds get everywhere. The bane of my life as an urban gardener.

Highfalutin title, actually. All I've got is a window box.

~

Len Saculla's Biography

To his astonishment, Len Saculla has once been a Pushcart Prize nominee. He has recently been published at *Speculative 66* (USA online SF and horror magazine). He has also featured in the Christopher Fielden adverb, sensory, nonsensical and preposition challenges.

107: THE NON-RHYMING COUPLETS OF ZAYN AND PERRY

by David Guilfoyle

Basically, at the end of the day, it is what it is. Simple as. I've been down this road before. It gets you nowhere fast. Crying over spilled milk, trying to be someone you're not, it's not big, funny or clever.

The thing is, life's too short. In the grand scheme of things, I know this is just small potatoes, but I've gone through this over and over again. I've got to get this off my chest. Before things take a turn for the worse.

The way I look at it is, me and you just aren't in it for the long haul. I can't put my finger on the why's and wherefores and, if I'm being honest, it's not you it's me. I just hope that when all is said and done we can still be friends.

~

David Guilfoyle's Biography

42 year old married father of two, lapsed marathon runner, failed five-a-side footballer, retired pub philosopher, currently injured, hence the tentative foray into writing.

108: DEAR DIARY

by Sandra Orellana

Look on the bright side, it could be easy for both of us. Today is the day.

With a lot of feelings, I will tear you apart into tiny pieces. For you, it was all a dream, but I can handle it. Little do you know, it is coming. You will be thrown into the trash.

You fell head over heels in love with me. But I am alive and well. I've decided to start writing to others, rather than you. Our bed of roses is a cold comfort.

Thank you for being my process of writing to the world. Another day, another hope for me. A sea of change is my new outlook. It will be as easy as pie for me to be free of you.

Good night forever. Let's sleep it off.

~

Sandra Orellana's Biography

Sandra Orellana is the author of *The Arch Of Surprises*. She enjoys writing short stories for Christopher Fielden. She is promoting her children's book and working on her second novel. She's an American living in Mexico City and San Miguel Allende.

www.amazon.com/Arch-Surprises-Sandra-Orellana/dp/1983552658/

109: A FROZEN MOMENT

by Ejder S. Raif

I'm standing in a busy building, the radiator as cold as ice, surrounded by several others, wrapped up warm to avoid freezing to death.

An old man bellowing, his voice as loud as thunder.

A group of children playing, as good as gold, while a group of workmen work their socks off, as they try to repair the heating.

A young lady with personal issues, hoping that there's light at the end of the tunnel.

A baby who normally struggles to sleep goes out like a light.

Hooray, the heating has finally been repaired. Everyone's as happy as Larry.

~

Ejder S. Raif's Biography

Ejder S. Raif has been published in *Boscombe Revolution*, NUHA Foundation's 2013 Blogging Prizes, and Christopher Fielden's writing challenges. He lives in London and works as a Student Support Worker. He volunteers as a web editor and content writer.

www.medium.com/@esraif

110: FROZEN IN TIME

by C.I. Selkirk

It was all going up the proverbial creek. Sure, it was as easy as taking candy from a baby, so long as the baby wasn't screaming the house down and the candy wasn't my phone playing 'Frozen' on repeat. Daddy's girl had me between a rock and a hard place. Taking it would be like pulling teeth and I'd get nowhere fast. If I let her keep it, her mother would say I was spoiling her rotten and that would be another black mark in her book. There were no winners or losers, it was how you played the game.

Just as I was at my wit's end, I was saved by the bell. The phone sang like a canary and in that split second when the apple of my eye didn't know if she was coming or going, I seized the day. I was on top. Case closed.

~

C.I. Selkirk's Biography

C.I. Selkirk searched high and low for clichés that really hit the mark while trying to maintain some semblance of dignity in front of friends and family but discovered they couldn't make a silk purse out of a sow's ear.

111: THERE'S A FIRST TIME FOR EVERYTHING

by Shirley Muir

When you turned up like a blast from the past, I feared you were flogging a dead horse – and were probably three sheets to the wind. I suspected we should let sleeping dogs lie, but you were determined to take the bull by the horns.

"I'm champing at the bit to spill the beans since the old man kicked the bucket," you said, happy as a sandboy. "His Will opened a can of worms." You looked like something the cat dragged in but were determined to talk turkey right from the off.

"Dad killed two birds with one stone," you said. "He wasn't poor as a church mouse, despite his down-at-heel shabbiness." Apparently we both have to get hitched before we can enjoy a life of Reilly with Dad's Rich-as-Croesus fortune.

We both pass muster – but hey, no pain, no gain.
There's plenty of fish in the sea.
Carpe diem.

~

Shirley Muir's Biography

Shirley Muir leaves no stone unturned in her search for the Holy Grail of fiction. She likes to push the envelope, doesn't rest on her laurels and knows that smart cookies don't crumble.

She sweated blood to produce this story.

112: THE TIME TRAVELLER'S LAMENT

by Robbie Porter

It seemed to last an eternity, but was really only a matter of time. Travelling faster than the speed of light took nerves of steel. He was as brave as a lion. Everyone he left behind was as old as the hills and he was as fit as a fiddle. That's relativity for you.

'All for one and one for all.' That's the motto at the Academy. But when the neuron drive failed, he was scared out of his wits and frightened to death. No one had survived such a catastrophic event before.

"The writing's on the wall," he mused. Then he remembered: what goes around comes around. He just had to connect with the supply ship when it passed through the portal.

He lost track of time, but the Large Magellanic Cloud had a silver lining: the supply ship, and just 99 years overdue.

In the nick of time.

~

Robbie Porter's Biography

Robbie Porter is a lecturer and charity worker from Worcester, England. He has released two collections of 100 word stories, available on Amazon.

113: PAIN IN THE NECK

by Claire Apps

What a pain in the neck. Who would have thought that crashing her car would have resulted in a metal pole sticking through her slender neck? She would have to pay through the nose to have her Porsche repaired – that was if it could be repaired. Well, she could well afford it. She wasn't as poor as a church mouse anymore. She had a pretty penny saved in her bank account.

She sat there unable to move, wondering if she would be pushing up the daisies soon, as no one seemed to be coming to help. Out of nowhere, a man appeared and, thanking her lucky stars, she had hope against hope of living again. She tried to speak but couldn't and then saw the axe in the man's hands as he raised it high and struck it downwards. He sure had an axe to grind. Nothing personal you understand.

~

Claire Apps' Biography

I teach Creative Writing to vulnerable women and I like writing poetry and sci-fi.

114: NEVER A BORROWER OR A LENDER BE

by Soulla Katsiani

What? Are you seriously going to bite the hand that feeds you?

Actions speak louder than words. I'd watch your step if I were you. Pride comes before a fall.

I know two wrongs don't make a right, but the pen is mightier than the sword.

By hook or by crook, I'll make you pay.

There is no such thing as a free lunch.

Please don't count your chickens before they hatch.

Fools rush in where angels fear to tread.

You have crossed a line.

And now I know a leopard can't change his spots, just as I know this worm's for turning.

No more Mr Nice Guy.

You're a wolf in sheep's clothing.

You obviously see me as a fool and his money to be easily parted.

But you sow what you reap and what goes around, comes around.

So I wish you well on your journey to hell.

~

Soulla Katsiani's Biography

Soulla Katsiani was born in North London to Greek Cypriot parents and is happily married with two daughters. She hasn't ventured far and still lives in North London.

115: SEASON FIVE SYNDROME

by Jake Kendall

"Victim is white, male. Cause of death... well, Ma'am, that's pretty obvious."

"What a blood-bath."

"Dismembered into 55 pieces. Most likely the homeowner, one Edward Richman, formally a successful and prominent banker. I guess he thought himself the best thing since sliced Ed."

"Goddamit, you're a professional pathologist, Darren. This is a time for respect, not puns."

"Sorry, Ma'am. Please don't sulk."

"I wasn't. I was just considering my tragic backstory. My husband worked in banking."

"I remember he had an affair and went suspiciously missing when you confronted him."

"Wait... why tip us off today? What's the date?"

"May fifth. Good lord, 55. Kinda."

"My husband's birthday."

"How convoluted. It's like the killer knows you personally. Again."

"We never found his body. Could this be him, toying with me from beyond the grave?"

"Everyone's a suspect."

"Agreed. I can't even rule out myself, thanks to this accursed amnesia."

~

Jake Kendall's Biography

Jake Kendall is a creative writing graduate of Cardiff University, currently living in his hometown of Oxford. He was recently included in *Here Comes Everyone, The Brutal Issue*.

116: GOODFELLAS

by Hannah Brown

"Is that all you've got?"

"I brought everything but the kitchen sink. I'm armed to the teeth." Tommy smiled, revealing a row of knives in his mouth.

"You're up the creek without a paddle." Alf started shuffling a deck of cards. "The writing is on the wall and I'm a happy camper. I'm holding all the cards."

"It's not whether you win or lose, it's how you play the game." Tommy pulled a long metal chain out of his back pocket, but it snapped in half.

"A chain is only as strong as its weakest link and that one's about as useful as a lead balloon," Alf replied smugly. "You couldn't hit the broad side of a barn."

"I've still got an axe to grind with you." Tommy smirked, brandishing a pickaxe in the air.

Alf picked up a hammer and grinned widely. "I'd prefer to bury the hatchet."

~

Hannah Brown's Biography

Hannah Brown is a not-very-professional writer, extremely talented background extra and a knitter of medium proficiency.

117: IN THE EYE OF THE STORM

by Abigail Williamson

Far, far away and long, long ago it was raining cats and dogs. Stella lost track of time. The downpour seemed to last an eternity. One day rolled into another. In the calm before the storm, Stella's life seemed clouds with silver linings. Now she saw just clouds.

Her father said, "It's better to have loved and lost, than to never have loved at all."

"Time heals all wounds," chipped in her mother.

Stella *had* been head over heels in love. No longer.

For weeks, she had the heart stopping, gut wrenching feeling she would never see dry land again.

"Water, water everywhere, nor any drop to drink," Stella murmured.

Time was running out. Stella felt the writing was on the wall.

Then, in a blink of an eye, the rain stopped. Just as suddenly as it had started.

The ark screeched to a halt.

~

Abigail Williamson's Biography

I am a nurse who enjoys short story fiction, classical music and writing.

118: HOW TO LIVE HAPPILY EVER AFTER

by Anita Goveas

If you could read between the lines, he was always on the verge of something: a better job, a publishing contract, success. But all that glitters is not gold and one man's meat is another man's poison. Why should he tie himself in knots?

It took three marriages, two therapists and a patient bartender to work out he was immersed in a story as old as the hills. He'd got used to living on the edge.

~

Anita Goveas' Biography

Anita Goveas is British-Asian, based in London, and fueled by strong coffee and paneer jalfrezi. She was first published in the *2016 London Short Story Prize Anthology*, most recently in *Dime Show Review* and *Literary Orphans*.

She tweets erratically: @coffeeandpaneer

119: BACK AGAINST THE WALL

by Jack Evans

It was the moment of truth. After working on it 24/7 and pulling an all-nighter, Tim's fate was now sealed.

Professor John Smith entered the room, his white-washed hair and flapping laboratory coat trailing behind him. He placed the report on the desk and sipped on his cup of tea, before shooting a disapproving look. Tim knew that some pearls of wisdom would be delivered.

"I am afraid to say your grammar is extremely poor and this is just the tip of the iceberg. We need to address the issue. Bottom line, as a ball park figure, you haven't scored more than 30. It boggles the mind, it is not rocket science."

Tim looked up meekly. "You're always moving the goalposts," he stammered.

"I know that you can do better. We won't beat around the bush. We all need to be singing from the same hymn sheet."

~

Jack Evans' Biography

Jack Evans is an 18 year old undergraduate science student. He enjoys reading thrillers, gardening and writing creative pieces for competitions / challenges in his spare time.

120: WHAT A LILY

by Gaius Rew

Keith saw her from across the bar and it was love at first sight. Her name was Lily. He couldn't gild her, and that man with her, Victor, was built like a brick house. A good one. The thorny issue to Keith was Victor treating Lily like a rose, though by another name she still smelled nice.

Keith knew he would have to reinvent the third wheel. If he wanted to jump her bones, he'd have to jump in with both feet without jumping the gun or jumping down her throat.

Lily held all the cards, so he'd have to play his cards right and keep them close to his chest, though he did have an ace up his sleeve where, as sure as the nose on his face, he wore his heart.

Lily looked to Keith and bit her lip. Keith bit his tongue. To Victor went the spoils.

~

Gaius Rew's Biography

I've always been full of words which wanted to come out, but I've never committed to sharing them. I hope somebody enjoys this particular combination I've decided on today. Full time doer of nuclear science, first time author of words.

121: THINKING OUTSIDE OF THE BOX

by Nam Raj Khatri

My mind was all over the place. Nothing was crystal clear. I was trying to think outside of the box.

Looking on the bright side, an idea came. It became brighter and brighter – the apple of my eye.

I wanted to share it with my nearest and dearest, but no one appeared. I looked as far as the eye can see.

A beautiful lady appeared. I was all ears. What was her name? A rose by any other name would smell as sweet. I shared my idea at the last minute. She took it well. All's well that ends well.

My dream ended, my mind came back down to earth and this story became ready to share.

~

Nam Raj Khatri's Biography

I am an environmental engineer from Nepal. Interested in art, photography and story writing.

www.facebook.com/namrajk

122: DAYLIGHT ROBBERY

by Lindy Gibbon

"The thing is, Nick, only time will tell if we're gonna get away with it."

Nick stared at his father, a giant of a man with a heart of gold. "But, Dad, surely, in this case, the writing's on the wall?"

Nick's dad – as tall as he was broad – glanced around the gloomy dimness of the subway and noted the graffiti daubed across the tiles. "Smart as a fox, you are, my boy. But, I can tell, you're frightened to death as well."

Nick, so scared he trembled like a leaf, when all was said and done, could only nod in agreement. "Gi' us an 'and then."

Father and son, dressed like council workers with hi-vis jackets and hard hats, carefully chiselled off the Banksy from the underpass wall.

"That's money in the bank right there, son."

They sprinted off at the speed of light.

~

Lindy Gibbon's Biography

Lindy Gibbon lives in Somerset where she spends her time writing, cooking and quilting. It's a hard life but someone's got to do it.

123: WINNERS NEVER QUIT, QUITTERS NEVER WIN

by KJ Walters

"Isn't it ironic?" my seatmate whispers.

The plane is going down like a hot potato. I'm texting like a banshee to friends and foes, loves and labours lost. I listen with half an ear. My seatmate doesn't see the forest for the trees.

"Ironic, isn't it?" she whispers again, her glass half empty. She thinks repetition is the cure to end all cures.

As we sink like a stone, I glance over. Sweat pours off her like water under the bridge. I smile. "We're done like dinner," I answer. "Our cookie's crumbled."

"I was always afraid of flying," she says. We hug it out.

"The sun has set on this life," I say.

"Don't throw out the baby with the bath water," she says. "It's still a horse race."

I nod. "Let's fight to the finish."

We watch with the patience of Job, as the minutes stretch like hours.

~

KJ Walters' Biography

KJ Walters works and writes in Victoria, BC, Canada. She loves wordplay, black comedy and tragedy. Poetry can be found everywhere. Spoken word on paper, micro fiction her muse.

124: A SWEET TOOTH

by Johanna McDonald

I have suffered at his hands for as long as I can remember. He was a thorn in my side from the year dot and he made my life a misery.

One day, he pushed me too far. I couldn't take any more. I snapped. He had clearly underestimated me and was about to find that he had met his match.

I decided to teach him a lesson he would never forget. After all, what goes around, comes around. An eye for an eye and all that. I wanted to make him wish that he had never been born and vowed to hunt him to the ends of the earth.

Anyway, now he's swimming with the fishes because, at the end of the day, revenge is sweet and I have got a very sweet tooth.

~

Johanna McDonald's Biography

I'm 48 years old, live in Hampshire with my little brown dog and work as a nurse in a local doctor's surgery.

125: A TALE OF THE WILD WEST

by John Notley

One-eyed Pete kicked open the bat wing doors of the saloon and surveyed the room, a gun in each fist. He eyed the customers, most of them hiding under tables, and stood toe to toe with the nearest man.

"I know you're here," he shouted, "you lily-livered, yellow-bellied, double-dealing son of a gun. Come outside and take your punishment like a man. This one-horse town ain't big enough for both of us. You're lucky the Sheriff ain't here. He'd hang you high, so I gotta do the dirty work myself."

"Steady on, old chap," the limey bartender interrupted. "Watch your tongue, there are ladies present."

"My trigger finger's itching, so get on your horse and ride off into the sunset before I lose my patience. If you don't come out now, you'll end up buzzard food in the bone orchard, pushing up the daisies."

~

John Notley's Biography

A retired travel agent, now having time on his hands, has taken up his pen again with the intent to shake up the world of literature. Only time will tell when the Grim Reaper will get his hands on him.

126: MY CHEERLEADER DREAMCAKE

by Jamie Martin

She didn't know it, but she was the light of my life.

As she walked through the school doors, my heart jumped into my mouth. Her smile could light up a room.

Unfortunately, Braden soon followed. Her boyfriend. Smirking slightly, he took her by the waist as they walked the halls together, his eyes darting elsewhere while she saw only him. He had 'player' written all over him...

They wandered in my direction. As the scent of her golden-blonde hair hit my nostrils, I couldn't help but breathe in. Wonder what would happen, without Braden. I could treat her so much better. I could be her lighthouse, the leader to her cheer. She could be my world.

Then, the class bell rang, breaking me out of my stupor. Off to biology, where she would be and I could content myself with staring at her across the room once more...

~

Jamie Martin's Biography

Hello there. I'm Jamie, a 15 year old kid writing relatively mediocre stuff. I'm your typical North West England nerd – horrific accent, constantly complaining about the weather, hiding behind books to avoid chavs. Enjoy my latest ball of I-wrote-this-in-an-hour-and-am-not-sure-what-I'm-doing.

127: BAKER'S DOZEN – UNLUCKY FOR SOME

by Christopher Fielden

Bernard Baker was as big as a house. Long ago, he'd mastered the art of cooking his award-winning Duodecuple Chocolate Muffin. It contained more sugar and fat than most bakers knew what to do with.

Despite being a master of his craft, Bernard always baked an extra muffin, on the off chance one would go awry. His cooking was near perfect, so every day he would eat a breakfast of champions – the 13th muffin.

Doctor Foster said, "Bernard, you'll end up in an early grave."

"What doesn't kill you makes you stronger," Bernard replied. His secret family recipe was too much to resist. He couldn't say no. Stuffing his face was the only option.

Of course, the inevitable happened – Bernard carked it. By now, he'd be pushing up the daisies, if he hadn't demanded to be buried at sea, with his friends Brian Butcher and Clive Candlestick-Maker.

~

Christopher Fielden's Biography

Chris writes, runs a humorous short story competition, plays drums and rides his motorcycle, sometimes to Hull. And back again.

He runs a multitude of writing challenges and has published 1,000s of authors in support of charity.

www.christopherfielden.com

128: THE IMPRESSIONIST

by Valerie Griffin

François Monnay, AKA Herbert Grimshaw, is an ambidextrous painter who's left hand doesn't know what his right is doing. After a hard day's night, he feels like metaphorically abandoning ship and going back to the drawing board. Having reached an impasse with his labour of love, he now finds himself well and truly stuck between a rock and a hard place.

At the end of his tether and having worked his fingers to the bone, François takes a step back from his painting, giving himself a bird's eye view. Hmmm. To be honest, it wasn't cutting the mustard. So much for coming on in leaps and bounds. He dabbed more paint onto the shiny rosy-red apples but it was too late, they'd already gone pear-shaped.

~

Valerie Griffin's Biography

Valerie is a published flash fiction and short story writer. She lives in Weymouth and hobbies include growing weird shaped vegetables and people watching on the seafront. Her first novel is under construction.

Find Valerie on Twitter: @griffin399

129: CLIMBING A MOUNTAIN

by Kathryn J Barrow

"So, going forward, I'm only gonna say 100%," I said, sweat dripping from my forehead.

"Don't get your knickers in a twist about it," Tom said. "Because, at the end of the day, if it ain't broke don't fix it."

It's an uphill battle for us getting up to Clifton. I stopped to catch my breath. "Hold on a minute. First, you tell me off for sayin' I'll give it 110%, cos it just ain't possible. Now, it don't matter?" I said. We continue to the top.

"It wouldn't be right if you stopped sayin' it. Everything you do is 110%. It'd be like eating a cherry pie with no cream. I mean, how wrong is that?"

"Well then, I'm still giving the band my 110%."

"And that's the writing on the wall, Harry, just the way it should be," he said, taking the final step to our destination.

~

Kathryn J Barrow's Biography

Kathryn grew up in a small village, left home at 16 and built a career in retail. Then, at 29, she found the confidence to study part-time completing an open degree, concentrating in design and creative writing.

130: SHUT YOUR TRAP

by Rhianna Gately

Once upon a time, a princess was locked in a tower and destined to be rescued by a tall, dark, handsome hero; a tale as old as time, if you will. So, this man (built like a tank) does the usual jack of all trades act: rides the horse, fights the dragon, etc. But I won't bore you to death. I'll skip to the good bit.

Reaching the top of the tower, he finds there's no door. So, he's banging his head against a brick wall until there's a chip in the old block and it all comes crashing down.

The princess gives a sigh of relief and explains how a good man is hard to find.

Suddenly, our hero finds it hard to swallow. It turns out there's a frog in his throat, which hops out of his mouth, kisses the princess and steals her heart.

~

Rhianna Gately's Biography

As an education studies student at university, I have the intention of becoming a teacher, but the aspiration of becoming a children's author. Imagination is always there, it just needs a bit of exercising, which is why I enjoy writing.

131: PULLING POWER

by David McTigue

Andy's eyes were on stalks.

"Don't fancy yours much," he said to Derek.

"The fiery redhead or the dumb blonde?"

"Either. Come on, let's strike while the iron's hot, and they're hot to trot."

Derek hesitated. "Mutton dressed as lamb," he quavered.

"You're as nervous as a kitten. Come on, let's do this."

The two lads set their stall out.

"What are you having?" asked Andy.

The blonde rolled her eyes. "A nervous breakdown."

"Do you come here often?" stammered Derek.

"Once every Preston Guild," answered Redhead, fluttering her eyelashes.

Derek grinned like a Cheshire cat, but the smile was wiped from his face when he was lifted by the scruff of the neck by a colossus.

Andy made his excuses and ran like the wind.

Derek cried like a baby.

Blondie laughed. "Put it down, Shep, you don't know where it's been."

~

David McTigue's Biography

Retail manager in real life, currently working in warehouse. Wife, three kids and a broken back.

132: EDD

by Ian Richardson

"Edd, get out of there, that whole place is rigged to blow in ten seconds. The McGuffin is a massive bomb."

Ten.

"Roger that."

Nine.

"Edd. Don't play God, it's too dangerous."

Eight.

"It's what I do. Danger is my middle name. Do I cut the red wire or the blue wire?"

Seven.

"We don't have a manual for that, Edd. You can still save yourself. Run."

Six.

"Over my dead body. I'm going to cut the red wire... see you in Hell."

Five.

"Edd, we've got everything crossed for you."

Four.

"I'm opening up this can of worms. Oh, oh... this is a proper soup sandwich."

Three.

"What's wrong, Edd?"

Two.

"All the wires are the same colour."

One.

"Edd?"

Zero.

"Edd..."

"Ah, it's OK... there was an off switch inside."

"Bravo Zulu, Edd."

"Just doing my job."

~

Ian Richardson's Biography

Ian has been reading books and comics for a long time. Eventually, inevitably he began to write and gained the confidence to share his work publicly. Ian lives on the East coast of Scotland.

133: A SHOT IN THE NOIR

by Maddy Hamley

The grizzled detective took a generous gulp of bourbon, peering over at the dame who'd walked into his office like she was trouble.

"So, detective," she purred. "That's the long and short of it."

"Piece of cake," the detective growled. "But what's your beef with Mr White?"

She sauntered to the window, smoke coiling from her long cigarette. "Burned the wrong bridges, didn't pay his dues, then flew the coop. It's payback time."

"White's a cool customer. He won't come quietly."

"Oh, he'll face the music." The dame's lip curled. "I've got an ace up my sleeve."

"Well, sorry to rain on your parade, sweetheart."

Her eyes widened at the Derringer pointed at her face. The detective grinned, lifting a cigar to his mouth. "Mr White, at your service."

~

Maddy Hamley's Biography

Maddy Hamley should be getting on with her PhD, but spends far too much time writing Twitter fiction as @nossorgs and sampling single-malts with her husband. Her work can be found in *Sensorially Challenged Volume 1*, *Tritely Challenged Volume 1*, or *Drabbledark*.

134: A FAIR COP

by Cathy Cade

It was hot as blazes. Flies circled my drink like bees around a honeypot. Charlie came out.

"We've another call, Blondie. No rest for the wicked."

Charlie gunned the air-conditioned estate, and we were briefed on the way. We joined the other squad car, cool as cucumbers and already up to speed. The fugitives had supposedly run into a copse, but I smelled a rat and made a beeline for gardens nearby.

On seeing me, one runaway broke cover and ran like the hounds of hell were chasing. I took off like a bullet from a gun as his mate stood up looking sick as a parrot.

The runner yelled like a stuck pig as I took him down. Charlie ran up with the bracelets and the team all gave me a pat on the head. Then Charlie threw my favourite ball and I was off again, like a rocket.

~

Cathy Cade's Biography

Cathy is an ex-librarian whose writing was formerly limited to instruction leaflets and annual reports. Now retired, she produces a different type of fiction, which has, so far, been published in *Scribble* and shortlisted in two competitions.

www.cathy-cade.com

135: WENDY OF THE WANDERERS

by Alan Barker

"She picks up the ball on the halfway line. She's in acres of space, she really does turn up in those quality areas... She's hugging the touchline, with two United defenders for company... She sells a dummy and leaves them for dead...

"Big Bertha slides in with a scything challenge. She glides effortlessly past...

"Now she's bearing down on goal, going for the jugular... She shapes as if to shoot, but instead plays a peach of a ball out to the wing... She's looking for the return... And – she – absolutely – buries – it.

"Wow, that goal was right out of the top drawer. The keeper never got a sniff... And the referee has blown up.

"It finishes 5-4 to Wanderers. You just couldn't write a script like this... This girl is really going places, she's got quality written all over her... Roy of the Rovers, eat your heart out."

~

Alan Barker's Biography

I am a retired tax accountant looking to fulfil a lifetime's ambition of writing stories and having them published. I recently completed a creative writing course. I am married and live in Epsom, Surrey.

136: TOO DARN HOT

by Jay Bee

Jake slouched onto the couch. "He's outside, under the umbrella, a jolly brolly," he'd muttered under his breath.

The waiter brought him a warm beer. One slurp and he hit the snooze button, and his eyes clanged shut. He didn't notice the tables filling up. Conversations drifted, trickling like treacle through his hot head.

"He died, you know. Deader than a doornail."

"Oh, my god, the Wi-Fi – free for three years."

"Went away to, err, find 'imself. Came back as hand luggage."

"It stopped working, just like that."

"Mustn't speak ill of the dead."

"Too good to be true, I suppose. And I broke my toe, sticks and stones..."

"We missed the funeral. They said no one waxed lyrical."

"Right pain in the neck."

"Ta ra, take care, you two. See you."

"Patience is a virtue, but not... Oh, look. It's... our Jake."

~

Jay Bee's Biography

Jay enjoys experimenting with words.

137: THE QUEST

by Angela P Googh

The remains of a 150-year-old stone and mortar wall is foundation for rusted and broken wrought iron fencing. The evergreen hedge had long ago been suffocated by wild bushes and trees, and an un-harvested hay field has replaced the once proudly manicured lawn. The only sign of manicuring now is the town-enforced shearing where the micro-woodland butts against the sidewalk.

Of the once grand home, its beauty is long gone. The lore at the local primary school has the owner feeding children to her many cats.

A young warrior has stealthily reached the door and, lifting a shaking arm, reaches out to ring the doorbell. *Thud.* A large Persian jumps onto the sill of a nearby window. Our hero's heart skips a beat as he turns to escape, coming within a few feet of an old woman waving her cane menacingly.

The lore, it breathes and lives on.

~

Angela P Googh's Biography

Angela P Googh is a computer programmer by profession. She is married with two grown children, active in her church, an amateur genealogist, and green except for her thumbs. Angela lives in Waterloo, Ontario, Canada.

Find Angela on Twitter: @angelagoogh

138: THE APPOINTMENT

by Sarah Wilde

"Not enough room to swing a cat in here," she said loudly, squinting around the room. Rose settled her ample body into a chair, brushing tabby hairs off her skirt.

"Still, at least it's dry. It's raining cats and dogs out there. Sit down, Fred," she said sharply. "It looks like you've got ants in your pants."

"Yes, dear."

She nodded at a mousy lady across the room. "Wonder if her snake of a husband is back yet," she muttered darkly. "It's like the elephant in the room at church and we're all tiptoeing around it."

"Really?" Fred managed, feebly. "Was he that bad?"

"I just tell it as I see it. He was always a bit of a dark horse."

Just then, the vet burst into the room, strutting like a cockerel. "Tiddles? Come on in."

"Yes please," Rose replied. "There are far too many animals out here."

~

Sarah Wilde's Biography

Sarah likes to spend time adventuring, writing and taking photos. She lives on a river in sunny Devon and has a blog about family life on a boat at:

www.sarahontarquilla.blogspot.com

139: NOVEL

by A.H. Creed

At the back of a stockroom, three editors sit around a table. There is a furtive air about them, but it's ink not nicotine that stains their fingers.

The first man drops a pack of corner-stapled paper onto a similarly-stapled pile on the table. "Switched at birth," he says.

The second man slaps down a manuscript, saying, "I'll raise your switched-at-birth, with a feisty raven-haired beauty."

A much thinner pile lands. The woman says, "The detective was the killer."

"Hmmm," they say. There doesn't seem to be a clear winner.

"Last go," first-man says, stealing a glance at the door. Drop. Thud. "Amnesia," he says.

"Hah," dismisses second-man, upping the ante with, "Tomboy princess who refuses to marry the prince."

The woman chews her lip. She shuffles papers. She slips something from the bottom of the pack.

"Pay up, boys," she says, as she goes all-in with, "Evil identical twin."

~

A.H. Creed's Biography

I am dyslexic, I can't spell. Don't know my commas from my colon, which means I don't write well. But sometimes I write unique, and sometimes I write funny. So I might write *Sixty Shades*, and make loads of money.

140: CLICHÉ TOWN

by Steven Barrett

Being the sheriff of Cliché Town is a tough job, but someone has to do it.

I'd vowed to move Heaven and Earth to maintain law and order and a high level of clichés in the town.

I looked around my office. I'd had a revolving door installed, and since then, I didn't know if I was coming or going.

I remember when things were different. I'd been an outlaw from the wrong side of the tracks. But one day, I arrived in Cliché Town and thought, *if you can't beat 'em, join 'em*. My new life as the Cliché Kid began.

After a few years, I became the sheriff. I remember the previous sheriff's words on his deathbed. "You don't have to be mad to work here, but it helps."

Now, I fight alongside my good friend, Doc 'I need a holiday just to get over my' Holliday.

~

Steven Barrett's Biography

Steven was born and lives in Edinburgh. He tries to keep fit by running and enjoys entering races, because it's not the winning but the taking part that counts.

141: THE OCCASION I SOMEHOW PASSED MY GEOGRAPHY EXAM DESPITE HAVING NO SENSE OF DIRECTION

by Mike Scott Thomson

Halfway through the test, my mind goes completely blank. A brain like a sieve, that's my problem. Everything in one ear, out the other. Sweat beads on my forehead. I'll have to repeat the year, no doubt.

I stare at the map on the answer sheet. 'Label the rivers.' Scaling the North Face of the Eiger would've been easier. At least I know that's in Wales.

I take a sneaky peak up. Everyone else is beavering away. Could I catch a glimpse? No way, José. Cheats never prosper.

Yet, hope springs eternal, as the Pope once said. Must give it my best shot. Eyes down. Nose to the grindstone. And…

One week later, I get the shock of my life.

"I passed?"

"Despite your rabbit-caught-in-headlights look," the teacher says, "it seems you DO know your Ouse from your Elbe."

Guess I'll take that as a compliment.

~

Mike Scott Thomson's Biography

Mike Scott Thomson's short stories have been published by journals and anthologies, plus have won the occasional award, including first prize in Chris Fielden's inaugural To Hull And Back competition.

Based in south London, he works in broadcasting.
www.mikescottthomson.com

142: JUNIOR'S DAD

by Justine Quammie

The apple doesn't fall far from the tree.

As a young boy, Junior grew up wanting to step into his father's footsteps. He practiced talking like him and even pulling up his trousers like his dear old dad. Every day, he would look in the mirror and repeat the affirmation, "I am the champion. I am a winner. I'll be like my daddy by dinner."

His father would walk him to and from the bus stop. When they played baseball together, his dad would say, "Junior, you're a right chip off the old block," as he play boxed with him.

Nights would fly by like this until his mother, Martha, came into the yard. In a high pitched voice, she would say, "John, dear? You and Junior come into the house for dinner."

Junior always knew his dad was the greatest dad in the whole wide world. Yes, siree Bob.

~

Justine Quammie's Biography

My poetry name is Travelling Roots (and my government name is Justine Q.B.). I live in Washington, DC, USA where I teach English language arts as a way of feeding my love of luxury and comfort.

Instagram handle: @forloveofwriting

143: ENOUGH IS ENOUGH

by Valerie Fish

"Once a cheater, always a cheater," my best friend delighted in telling me. She was right of course; a leopard never changes his spots.

I should have seen it coming but they do say love is blind. I thought I'd found my knight in shining armour, I fell for his charms hook, line and sinker. I was putty in his hands.

When I confronted him, he didn't bat an eyelid, looked at me as if butter wouldn't melt in his mouth.

This time, his cock and bull story didn't wash with me; he'd led me down the garden path once too often with his lies and shenanigans.

No way, José, enough was enough.

At the end of the day, there are plenty more fish in the sea. So, I showed him the door, but not before hitting him where it hurts – literally.

~

Valerie Fish's Biography

Valerie has had a love of the English language since her school days, inspired by a fantastic English teacher. She likes to 'write from the heart' and hopes that's reflected in her work.

144: WHY ME?

by Lee Kull

I used to be high on the hog, happy as a clam. Now, I'm down on my luck, in the pits, and everybody asks, "Why the long face?" They should walk a mile in my shoes…

I got fired. My car got towed, so I walked home, only to find an eviction notice on my door. Walking inside, I tripped over the body of my dead dog. Stumbling into the kitchen, I found a letter:

Dear John, I ran off with the milkman. Love, Susan.

At a bar, drowning my sorrows, I told the bartender my woes. The seven-foot-tall buck-toothed hombre next to me wearing a sombrero, poncho and six-shooter, called me a liar. I shot him, because them's fightin' words. The police came and threw me in jail.

Now, I'm imprisoned for life, although I ain't done nuthin' wrong. I'm crying my heart out.

I really miss that dog.

~

Lee Kull's Biography

Lee Kull is an aspiring author with three books in progress: a Christian action/adventure novel, a collection of short stories, and an educational children's picture book. Lee's interests vary greatly, but reading, writing, and herbalism have always topped the list.

145: BODY SHOT

by Clare Tivey

The call came in at 21:15 and was the icing on the cake of a particularly hard day at the office for Detective Armstrong. Tired, and hungry as a horse, she responded. Body of an unidentified male, aged mid-20's. Another day, another shooting, or so she thought...

She would drive by and collect her new partner, Andy, a rookie who was pleasant enough but very eager to please.

On arrival at the scene, forensics were still busy. The familiar metallic stench of blood hung in the air. Visibly pale, Andy put a hand over his nose and mouth. As she moved to enter the room, she stopped in her tracks at the doorway.

"Sarge, there's something you should know before you go in there."

With those words, she was immediately transported back to a case two years previously. The case that still haunted her to this day.

~

Clare Tivey's Biography

I live in Suffolk with my partner, Matt, enjoying the countryside, cycling and wild swimming. I write short stories for fun, and catharsis. My ambition is to have a whole book published one day.

146: OVERCOOKED IT

by Tony Thatcher

The wreckage from the mangled car lay strewn across the road like confetti. Same model as mine. Talk about there but for the grace of God.

The driver obviously hadn't honed his skills to my levels of perfection and had stuffed it. I'd been round that bend more times than I've had hot dinners, the massive V8 burbling angrily through twin exhausts, its gut-wrenching torque shredding the tyres as they scrabbled for grip, arms full of opposite lock keeping the mighty beast on the straight and narrow of the King's Highway.

But this guy had run out of road big time and now the emergency services were cutting open his pride and joy like a sardine can.

Nobody stopped me as I went over for a closer look. And nobody heard my anguished scream when I saw my bloodstained, lifeless corpse being zipped into a body bag.

~

Tony Thatcher's Biography

Most of my life has been spent designing stuff. When I'm not doing that, I write short stories and flash fiction. I am currently composing award acceptance speeches for my half-finished novel.

147: WORK SPEAK

by Lucy Morrice

"It is important to get everyone on board, engage with all stakeholders and remain jargon free, going forward. I didn't get where I am today by ducking and diving, whispering in corridors, hanging out by the water cooler. No, I put my nose to the grindstone, pulled up my socks, got my skates on and now I am top dog."

Had all my colleagues, hanging off the chairman's words, had frontal lobotomies?

This is not what I signed up for, working for the man, stuck in the rat race of global corporation and materialism. Perhaps they were all seduced by the thought of a suburban home with 2.4 children and a BMW in the driveway, but not me, I am a free agent.

I sprang to my feet, stripped myself of my restrictive office wear and streaked from the auditorium.

"I want to be a tree."

~

Lucy Morrice's Biography

Lucy Morrice likes flash fiction as it is manageable in a busy life. She lives in Scotland and writes from time to time.

148: A CLICHÉ MOMENT

by Janice Eileen Morris

It was raining cats and dogs, and I was feeling mighty blue,
   Waiting to hear the drop, of that dreaded other shoe.

Because my heart was broken, I'd become a couch potato,
   Drowning in a sea of grief, over the split with my tomato.

I'd been a grumpy bear that day, getting up on the wrong side of the bed,
   And I'd badly ruffled her feathers, with the hurtful things I'd said.

I should have bitten my tongue, which meant swallowing my pride.
   Now my stomach and my chest, both had butterflies inside.

It was a bitter pill to swallow, when I finally reached out to hold her,
   And she told me to get lost, giving me the cold shoulder.

I was on pins and needles, until she finally forgave me.
   Now it's water under the bridge, just a bad memory.

~

Janice Eileen Morris' Biography

I am an 84 year old widow who lives in a group home. I enjoy writing short stories and poetry as well as exploring the internet to see what others have written. This is my first entry to a competition.

149: WEATHER TALKS

by Valeria Lützow

The new girl, Gwyneth, was impossibly tall. She had to be larger than the players of the school's basketball team. Sage was so curious about her that he couldn't resist seeking her out during recess.

"Tell me, how is the weather up there?"

Gwyneth looked so exasperated that when she rolled her eyes, Sage was worried they would get stuck in her head.

"The same as it is for you, I imagine," she responded, before biting into her nice-looking cucumber sandwich.

"I don't know. I've never thought about it. Tell me, is it hard to find someone to date?"

"I'm 12. I don't think about dating."

"You're pretty boring for a girl."

"You're pretty nasty for a human being."

"Tell me, do you play basketball?" Sage was looking at her with curious eyes, and he seemed to feel no shame.

"Tell me, Sage, are you self-conscious about your height?"

~

Valeria Lützow's Biography

My name is Valeria Lützow, I am 18 years old and have had a soft spot for literature ever since I could read. I am currently working on a novel, which is pretty challenging since I write in self-taught English.

150: CLICHY CLICHÉ

by Munib Haroon

This muse was not amused. It was a cramped garret in the writer's block of flats in Paris. The bed was occupied. She knew he'd be up at the crack of dawn, but the consumptive cough was consuming him. She had to inspire before he expired.

Why do I get the hard ones? The other muses get authors sipping lattes in coffee shops.

She approached his desk. *Ugh, a mess… bottles of whisky, unpaid bills, a prescription for mercury and a challenge to a dusk duel from a Parisian duke. And a typewriter? It's 2018, for Zeus's sake.* Annoyed, she grabbed the bulky thing and tossed it across the room.

CRASH.

The writer woke up with a jolt. "What a fine bogey dream. I dreamt my typewriter exploded, blowing off my hands. I feel suddenly inspired."

The muse grinned like the Cheshire cat that'd got the cream.

~

Munib Haroon's Biography

Munib is a Paediatrician and medical editor who lives in Yorkshire.

151: BACK TO THE DRAWING BOARD

by Kathleen E Williams

Sara thought long and hard about putting herself out there again. She'd been on a wild goose chase for too long, like someone still wet behind the ears in the dating world.

"It's probably time I just take the bull by the horns and weather the storm instead of running in circles hoping love will find a way." Bob and she had had their moment in the sun until he'd pulled the wool over her eyes.

"He was a real snake in the grass," Sara admitted, "but that's water under the bridge. Today is the first day of the rest of my life," she proclaimed. "I'm putting my best foot forward, going out on a limb and meeting Lucy's newly available friend."

Later, when her doorbell rang, Sara was dressed to kill. All thumbs, she opened the door, smiled before she looked up and choked out, "BOB?"

~

Kathleen E Williams' Biography

Kathleen Williams, recently retired from a 25-year teaching career and 35- year marriage, is beginning to share a lifetime of stories and eccentricities in publication. This lifetime Chicagoan visits her children and grandchildren in warmer climates.

linkedin.com/in/kathleen-williams-9a18b655

152: YOUNG AT HEART

by Helen Fawdon-Rochester

Bored to tears with watching daytime television, Doris decided to look for a job. Over the hill but still young at heart, Doris realised nothing ventured nothing gained as she entered the job centre. She knew that beggars couldn't be choosers at her age, when it came to finding a job.

At 84, she was no spring chicken, but she was up with the larks and looking as fresh as a daisy and eager to go to work.

Working like a dog to keep the wolf from the door, she wasn't wet behind the ear. She knew how to earn an honest crust. After all, the job was easy as pie, working in the pastry factory.

~

Helen Fawdon-Rochester's Biography

I live in Northumberland with my pets. I enjoy reading crime thrillers and writing short stories. After seeing my name in print via a previous challenge, it inspired me to write for another. It's fun and raises money for charity.

153: YOU CAN'T TURN THE CLOCK BACK

by Maggie Elliott

Out of the blue, my ex-girlfriend turned up at my flat like a bad penny.

I dropped a right clanger by telling her she looked like she had been dragged through a hedge backwards.

She said she felt as rough as a badger's bottom.

She hadn't slept a wink for days since her new beau told her to take a hike.

Her name was Primrose, but clearly she'd been on a bender. She smelt like a brewery.

I gave her a sweet tea then showed her the door, telling her, "You dropped me like a hot potato weeks ago. Well, now your chickens have come home to roost. On your bike."

She wailed like a banshee as she left with her tail between her legs.

~

Maggie Elliott's Biography

Maggie Elliott is a retired PA who lives in Oxfordshire and writes purely for pleasure. She loves animals, particularly cats, and watching old fashioned television comedies.

154: ALL THE CLICHÉS ONE STORY CAN HAVE

by Rima El-Boustani

All that glitters isn't gold, my friend. Read between the lines, this money isn't yours, it's mine. In the nick of time, I see the truth.

Only time will tell if you worked enough, these past few days. Your tail between your legs, you go about begging for money at banks and on the streets to boot. Every cloud has a silver lining, but very few are made of gold. When life gives you lemons, make lemonade and sell it for more. Your knickers are twisted if money is not what you want. Cat got your tongue?

You got up on the wrong side of bed and stepped on something that was left there. This time it wasn't money, but the dog's poo. We're not laughing at you, we're laughing with you. I swear.

And so, with riches in coins and paper and cheques, they lived happily ever after.

~

Rima El-Boustani's Biography

Rima is a prolific writer who enjoys many genres and loves to push her skill. Writing takes her into a different world, where anything and everything can happen.

155: I'M NOT GETTING TOO OLD FOR THIS

by K. J. Watson

"You're a dinosaur, a fish out of water," N told me.

"Au contraire," I replied. "You still need agents like me to find the bad guys and terminate them with extreme prejudice."

N sniggered.

I continued, "Didn't I stop a manic billionaire from closing an orphanage this morning?"

"No, you did not," N said. "You were dozing like a baby at your desk. You dreamt you saved an orphanage."

To be fair, N had me bang to rights.

"Wait," I said triumphantly. "There's a box attached to your desk. See? It's got a clock and coloured wires."

"A bomb?" N asked, trembling like a jelly.

"With 10 seconds until detonation," I answered, producing a pair of wire cutters.

"Do the necessary," N commanded.

"Oh, now you need me," I said, somewhat smugly. "Well, I only have to cut the red wire."

"The red?"

"It's always the red. Here we go."

~

K. J. Watson's Biography

I am a copy editor and online content writer. My occasional fiction includes scripts for a comic and annual (some while ago) and stories for young children. I live near Loch Lomond with my wife and two dogs.

156: THE HAIRDRESSER

by Jill Sunter

The alarm, although expected, still managed to jar Trevor. His stomach knotted as he stretched over and hit the button, silencing the deafening noise. He would give anything to be able to roll over and slide back into his dream of Bobby Ewing stepping out of the shower.

Suddenly, his face screwed up as he realised it was Saturday – the longest day of the week. His customers in the hair salon were always far harder to please. Ladies wanting to be as beautiful as flowers for nights out, which he always pictured ending in disaster. Middle-aged women wearing sparkly tops, drinking too many white wine spritzers and ending up with their head down a toilet.

He shuddered involuntary.

If only something different could happen. Unexpectedly, like a bolt out of the blue, there was a knock at the door.

~

Jill Sunter's Biography

Jill Sunter lives and writes in Fife, Scotland. If she isn't writing, reading or drinking wine she is sleeping. She has a novel available to download from Amazon and is currently working on her second novel.

www.amazon.co.uk/Same-Individuals-Jill-Sunter-ebook/dp/B006ZVN2CQ

157: AFTER THE FUNERAL

by Richard Betton-Foster

Jack: Poor old Fred, pushing up the daisies now from six feet under.

Pete: Knew 'is dad, salt of the earth. Our Fred, chip off the old block, eh?

Jack: No flies on Fred. Always the life and soul of the party. The tales he'd tell. Had me in stitches; I'd laugh like a drain.

Mark: But he'd not suffer fools gladly.

Jack: No way. Great bloke, reliable. Always count on his support. With his back to the wall he'd put his best foot forward to help.

Pete: Yeah, stiff upper lip and all.

Mark: Did so much for the town. Unsung hero if ever there was one.

Jack: Dunno about that. John's eulogy praised him to high heaven.

Me: Put a sock in it, or we'll all be talking like this till the cows come...

(Exit, pursued by a bear.)

~

Richard Betton-Foster's Biography

Born 1943 in Guildford. As architect, practised in London, Brighton and Yeovil. Married in 1985. Ran guesthouse in Wells from 1997, then retired in 2012 to small house near Sherborne. Still alive – just.

158: ON THE WRONG TRACK

by Paul Mastaglio

"Do you know where you're going?" Susan despaired. "You can't see the wood for the trees."

"Well, it was raining cats and dogs before," John replied.

"How long is this walk going to take?"

"How long is a piece of string?"

"Are you saying we're lost?" Susan cried.

"Not exactly. We'll get there in the fullness of time."

"We're lost."

"No, we've just got to take things one step at a time. Rome wasn't built in a day," emphasised John.

"You mean it's going to take longer than a day to get to the pub?" Susan wailed.

"Ah, you're always a glass half empty."

"Admit it. We're up the creek without a paddle."

"No, but I think we're between the devil and the deep blue sea."

"I'll ring Mountain Rescue," sighed Susan.

"Do you know roughly where we are?"

"Between a rock and a hard place."

~

Paul Mastaglio's Biography

Retired bank clerk who lives in North Tyneside with wife Yvonne and Toby the cat. Hobbies include archery, reading, walking.

159: SATURDAY MORNING HOUSE CLEANING

by James Louis Peel

It was child's play. But Bob couldn't wrap his head around house cleaning. He just couldn't win for losing. Every time he called a spade a spade, he only opened a can of worms.

His wife called the shots. She blamed him for being a bull in a china shop. He couldn't cut it and didn't stand a chance. No more channel surfing. His wife was ready to crack the whip. Bob knew she wouldn't call off the dogs, come what may. She was known for chewing nails and spitting out tacks.

He sensed a dog eat dog world. Would he cut and run? No, that wasn't Bob. He decided to crack down, use the charm offensive, cut to the chase, buy into it, change his tune and be as busy as a one-armed paper hanger come hell or high water while trying to cut the mustard.

~

James Louis Peel's Biography

James now lives in Japan, but is originally from Nicholasville, Kentucky. He is probably the only American who can speak Japanese with an Appalachian accent if required. Otherwise, he likes creating stories from the tangled bits of his varied experiences.

160: NOW THAT WAS THE QUESTION

by Rachel Heaton

She shouldn't be here. She was out of her league. Tears burned behind her eyes as she struggled to read the strange handwriting in front of her, then the words danced before her eyes. She couldn't even string a sentence together. She was messed up.

Everyone stared. Kind, sympathetic gaze. Don't lock eyes, soldier on, she could do this, she could read aloud the dancing words, tripping and slipping along the way. Did they see she was just a flash in the pan? A one trick pony? A walking disaster?

"Why are you here?" was the question asked by the teacher.

Why was she here? Now that was the question.

~

Rachel Heaton's Biography

Rachel Heaton writes stuff from her messed up brain. She is not popular, nor a nerd. She is someone flitting about gossiping and cackling. Rachel writes a column for a local rag – she thinks nobody reads it. She hopes nobody reads it.

161: THE CAT THAT GOT THE CREAM

by Beccy Golding

They were the golden couple.

Ruggedly handsome, with cheekbones to die for, Scott's eyes were so blue you could drown in them.

Cherry was the girl of his dreams. Her tiny waist, pert breasts and slim figure weren't all though – she wasn't just a pretty face. Cherry had the voice of an angel, a fierce intellect, and the maternal instincts of a lioness.

Together, Scott thought, they could conquer the world. With her brains and his brawn nothing could stop them, they had the world at their feet, everything to play for.

They'd met at the law firm – she'd tripped, papers tumbling across the floor. As he knelt to help, his fingers brushed hers. Their eyes met and time stood still; he thought he heard a nightingale sing. The world changed forever, things would never be the same again. He was truly the cat that got the cream.

~

Beccy Golding's Biography

Beccy Golding is a boring middle-aged woman. A time-wasting, wurzel-headed, button-muncher. She has the gall to think she can write pretty words, conjure up beauty, make bubbles of joy or lumps of sadness, somehow share her experience of being human.

162: WHEN LIFE GIVES YOU LEMONS

by Nichole Villeneuve

You could've knocked her down with a feather when Ruth found Gabe sitting at the back of the diner, looking down in the dumps. He was a regular – one you could set your watch by – who usually enjoyed eating his corned beef hash while perched at the front counter, amid the hustle and bustle.

"You looked a million miles away there, Gabe – like you've got the weight of the world on your shoulders."

"I've got a monkey on my back, Ruthie. I've bitten off more than I can chew, this time."

"It can't be as bad as all that. Wanna tell me what's eating you?"

"No, I'd bet my bottom dollar that you wouldn't understand."

"What am I, chopped liver? If life gives you lemons, make lemonade. We've all got our crosses to bear, so count your blessings, look on the bright side and finish your hash, honey."

~

Nichole Villeneuve's Biography

Nichole Villeneuve is a scientist, nature-lover and coffee addict, who sometimes writes books. When her lab coat comes off, she puts on her writer's cloak and crawls into her den, where she gets lost in creating worlds of romantic fiction.

163: A RECIPE FOR DISASTER

by Janet Pickett

Leaving his better half sleeping like a log, Arthur got on his high horse, bound for Merlin's smallholding. At the henhouse, he pulled a sling from up his sleeve and, killing two birds with one stone, he placed all their eggs in one basket. Ignoring a red herring, he snatched up a fine kettle of fish, then galloped away like a bat out of hell, pursued by the furious wizard.

His horse was frightened to death, and Arthur came down to earth with a bump.

Brandishing staves, the adversaries fought like tigers until Merlin got hold of the wrong end of the stick. Seizing his chance and the basket, Arthur ran like the wind.

Arriving home with neither fish nor fowl, he tried to use the broken eggs to make an omelette. Ravenous, Guinevere awoke, got out of the wrong side of the bed and dressed to kill.

~

Janet Pickett's Biography

Janet Pickett is a retired medical secretary. This is her first attempt at story writing.

164: SHOPPED

by Sean Bain

I'd been trailing the blonde bombshell down D aisle for some time now. She was a slippery customer and I was reeling her in, slowly but surely.

Butch Malloy always got his man, or woman. After all, I had a rep' to protect as store detective number one.

I saw her reach for the top shelf; it was going to be a long stretch. She stopped. Something wasn't right and she was clearly rattled. Maybe she could sense I was packing lead.

I played it cool and kept my distance. It was a game of cat and mouse and it wasn't too long before I caught her with her hand in the cookie jar.

She was all over the shop and flapped her gums in a heartbeat. I took down her particulars with the pencil from my pocket. This was one shopping trip that would cost her dearly.

~

Sean Bain's Biography

I am Sean Bain. I am 48, well-travelled, love writing, music, surfing, food, my cat and my wife, not necessarily in that order and I wish I'd tried harder at school... *Pffftt.*

165: A DOG'S LIFE

by Judy Reeves

Gary looked at me with that hangdog expression.

"Come on, Rover, it looks like I'm in the dog house again."

He and the missus, Sharon, had been at it hammer and tong since yesterday. I thought it was just a storm in a teacup and would soon blow over.

He dangled my lead and said, "Walkies."

It's a walk in the park, so yes please.

He could have talked the hind legs off a donkey, metaphorically speaking. I was all ears though.

He turned around and said, "We're the laughing stock of the estate. She walks around like mutton dressed as lamb."

Or a wolf in sheep's clothing, I thought.

"At the end of the day, she is a bit long in the tooth."

You're telling me.

He wasn't just barking up the wrong tree. A problem shared is a problem halved. After all, a dog is man's best friend.

~

Judy Reeves' Biography

I retired early from working in social care to concentrate on writing. I enjoy writing short stories, memoirs and recently discovered a talent for poetry too. I have completed a creative writing course with the Open University.

166: IDENTITY

by Khamis Kabeu

For a moment, I was transfixed. Finally, I decided always forward, never backward.

With bated breath and sweating like a pig, I reached the camp. As we prepared to sleep, sick as a dog, we heard people approach.

"Will you please identify yourselves before I blow you to shreds," barked our night watchman.

"Call off your dogs. I'm the chieftain," thundered their leader.

"Which chieftain?"

"You thick-headed fool. Who died and left you in charge?"

"It's an order."

"Shut up. We're looking for Khamis whom we fear might have been mauled by lions along the route to this outpost."

"Okeydokey."

"Woe unto you. Scared dogs bark most."

"You're a sitting duck, sitting on the fence, and stinking to high heaven."

"You are now swimming against the tide. If you don't take care of your knitting, I'll have you wag your tail between your legs," the chieftain said, and left.

~

Khamis Kabeu's Biography

I'm an up-coming creative writer of the short story and novel. I intend to specialise in the thriller genre, with women as my main characters. I live with my family in Malindi, on the Coast of Kenya.

167: NAIL IN THE COFFIN

by Daniel Purcell

On the stroke of midnight, things took a turn for the worse. This time, he really put his foot in it: instead of playing the tape of his soliloquy for the girl of his dreams, he mixed it up and played the incantations of *The Book of the Dead*, unearthing a multitude of sins. He'd planned it to a T, and it was meant to be a no-brainer. Now, he'd bitten off more than he could chew (and so would a few zombies).

Moon glimmering, he hurtled headlong through the dark forest like a bat out of hell (of which there would soon be many) and didn't see the branch, which would be the death knell for him. Why can't forest floors be trip-free of flotsam and jetsam when in a hurry?

He was a stone's throw from the haunted house on the hill when the hand grasped him.

~

Daniel Purcell's Biography

Daniel Purcell currently lives in Glasgow, Scotland. He has a BA in English from the University of Liverpool and has travelled extensively around the world. When he's not travelling, he enjoys writing and reading genre fiction (mainly horror and fantasy).

168: ASHLEY, MY LOVE AND MY SAVIOUR

by Raymond E. Strawn III

Homeless, he walked around without a care in the world. Life had been cruel. He was a diamond in the rough. All he needed was a chance to prove to the world that he was special. Only time would tell if he'd achieve his goals, or if it was all a waste of time.

On his journey, he met a girl. They were opposites. A rebellious city boy from the west coast, moving around his whole life, and a good country girl from the east coast, living in the same town her whole life.

With heart-stopping fear, he opened up to her and shared his gut-wrenching pain. She accepted him and fell head over heels in love with him. In the nick of time, she saved him from his pain. And he loved her more than life itself.

They lived happily ever after, with some occasional bumps on the road.

~

Raymond E. Strawn III's Biography

Raymond E. Strawn III began writing poetry and short stories in 1999. In 2001-2002, he spent 48 days wrongfully incarcerated for writing and sharing his poetry and short stories at his high school.

169: THE SECOND BUTTON

by Jessica Bowden

At the end of their high school graduation ceremony, Tetsuya pulls Asami aside to confess to her. His heart is pounding. They've been friends their whole lives. By confessing, he runs the risk of ruining their friendship, but if he doesn't, there's no doubt that someone will come along and sweep her off her feet in university. He doesn't want to have any regrets, so he takes a deep breath, musters up his courage, and tears the second button from the top of his blazer off.

"Will you accept this?" he asks, holding it out to her.

"You dummy." She smiles, her hazel eyes glistening with tears. Her neat, brown ponytail sways as she steps towards him. "What kind of question is that?" She takes the button from him. "Of course I'll accept it."

He sighs, happily, and holds her close. She fits against him like the perfect puzzle piece.

~

Jessica Bowden's Biography

Jessica is a writer who is absolutely fascinated with Japanese culture, thanks in part to anime and manga. She has years of experience with writing fanfiction, some of which she has admittedly used clichéd phrases and tropes to write.

170: DREAM BOY

by Tracey Maitland

Everybody needs something to work for, to get out of bed for, a ray of sunshine, light at the end of the tunnel, a glimmer of hope. You were mine.

Even the poorest guys on the street, who have nothing, have get up and go, a mission, a purpose and usually a smile on their faces. Why, when they have the hardest lives and it's survival of the fittest?

Is it because God gave them a purpose? They have no choice? They want to do better? They're driven? It's do or die?

Each day they wake up it's the same old slog, the same mountain to climb, the same story, just a different day.

I commend them. To face a relentless race, to be the first, best, fastest, fittest – against all the odds. They're superhuman, demi-gods, elite athletes in the race of life.

I've lived the dream too – *you.*

~

Tracey Maitland's Biography

"Life is either a daring adventure or nothing." (Helen Keller)

171: THE EXAM

by Josh Granville

You could hear a pin drop. But still it was as if the exam hall had feelings, jeering sarcastically.

Victorian architecture crumbling in academic failure. Overhead lights, glinting into the margins of my A4 lined paper. But they couldn't help me. They couldn't shine light on the situation. Only I could read between the lines. I had to work it out for myself. Even the two giant clocks, raised on pieces of cardboard packaging, told me it was my duty to think outside the box.

Having avoided revision like the plague, I'd now left it too late, shaking like a leaf on a wet winter's morning as raindrops of sweat plummeted to the ground.

I snatched my glasses off the table so I could look up at the clock, turning a blind eye to my incomplete exam. Half an hour left... I could do this.

~

Josh Granville's Biography

I am a young, creatively driven writer with a flair for words and waffling. I like to create humour and meaning through a play on words and experimentation.

172: TIME AND TIDE WAIT FOR NO MAN

by Gail Everett

Having lost track of time, Dad was taking an eternity to get ready, and didn't have a care in the world for the fact that we were running late.

I called him for the umpteenth time. "Dad, come on."

He shouted back at me, "Don't get your knickers in a twist, I'll be ready in two shakes of a lamb's tail – at the end of the day, it doesn't matter if we're five minutes late and, all things considered, I daresay we won't be alone."

"But Dad," I cried, "we're going to be about as popular as a fart in church if we're late for Uncle Jack's funeral."

"We're not going to church, it's the crem," said Dad. "Jack won't know, he's as dead as a doornail, and he'll be pushing up the daisies by teatime."

"You'd be late for your own funeral," I retorted. "Get a move on."

~

Gail Everett's Biography

Apart from what I told my mother when I was a teenager, my interest in fiction began at the tender age of 63, by which time I had exhausted most other possibilities for pastimes in which to engage whilst sitting down.

173: THE BUBBLEGUM POPPERS

by Rene Astle

"A toast to the success of an upcoming band," cried Mr Spheeris as he raised his glass of Coca Cola.

"The Bubblegum Poppers," everyone else agreed.

"The Bubblegum Poppers," laughed Mrs Cartwright.

"Cheers," they said together as they tipped their glasses.

With that word spoken, everybody drank their Coca Cola at great speed.

The Bubblegum Poppers got their first gig at Radio City Music Hall and were signed by G-Force Records to create 10 albums. Their managers, Mr Spheeris and Mrs Cartwright, weren't so sure they were gonna succeed until they heard the news.

"I can't believe it's happening so quick," said the lead singer, Max.

"Just think, guys," said the guitarist, Pauline, "our first album. We'll be the biggest band since The Beatles."

"Let's not get too carried away," said the second lead singer, Pam. "First, we have to make sure we get creative freedom for our new songs."

~

Rene Astle's Biography

Rene Astle is a talented artist and writer from New Zealand. He has a gallery of artwork for sale on ArtPal. His two published books are *What's So Funny? And Other Poems* and *Jumping Jupiter*.

www.reneastle.com

174: FOREVER POISED BETWEEN A CLICHÉ AND AN INDISCRETION

by Geoff Holme

"Damn and blast. I will *not* take this lying down. If there's one thing I can't abide, it's people poking their nose in where it's not wanted."

"Calm down, Foreign Secretary. It will soon blow over."

"A week is a long time in politics."

"We can weather the storm."

"I know your heart's in the right place and you mean well, but I'm caught between a rock and a hard place. The press will have a field day if they get hold of this. Promise me you won't breathe a word."

"What do you take me for, an idiot? You have my word. My lips are sealed."

"You're a brick. Where would I be without you?"

"Up the creek without a paddle. But just in case you take it into your pretty little head to throw me to the wolves, just remember this – I know where the bodies are buried."

~

Geoff Holme's Biography

Geoff is retired and therefore free to spend most of his time trying to improve his writing. In a previous life, he wrote over 300 SPAMericks – go on, Google it.

175: THE GOLDEN HAIRED BOY

by Selina Mignano

Golden hair, a perfect flair for leadership, all the girls by his side and a beautiful home life. You name it, Adrian had it all. After all, he was the chosen one, even at the tender age of 15.

His black school jumper fitted exquisitely around his already muscular shape. Adrian knew he had a knack for being simply perfect.

The aura of perfection in its rawest form even reached the minds of the higher-ups. Adrian had been chosen as a saviour as a result of a prophecy involving an evil wizard. Because of this, he was sent to an academy for gifted students of the Wicca Regime.

Despite being pushed into an environment he didn't know and having greatness thrust upon him, he somehow made a significant number of friends.

Little did he know that the peace he loved would eventually be shattered...

~

Selina Mignano's Biography

I am Selina Mignano, I am a second year university student and I enjoy fictional writing in my spare time. My favourite authors are Stephen King and Marcus Sedgwick.

www.selinawritersblog.blogspot.com

176: PRINCE WITH A P

by Alice Hale

Once upon a time there was a princess. Her father had locked her in a tower with a dragon to guard her. He was very overprotective of her.

The princess was lonely. She wished someone would rescue her from her tower.

Then, one day, someone came for her; a knight riding a beautiful white horse. Before the princess knew it, the dragon had been defeated and her rescuer had broken down her prison's door.

She saw a stretched out hand and heard the question she had wanted to hear ever since being locked away.

"Would you like to leave with me, princess Melody?"

She took the stranger's hand.

"I would love to. What is my saviour's name?"

Stormy blue eyes resembling sapphires seemed to look straight into her soul. "My name is Isabella Prince, though you may call me Isa if you wish," she said.

~

Alice Hale's Biography

Alice is a 17-year-old hobbyist writer from the Netherlands. She only started writing a couple of months ago. Her hobbies include reading, writing, listening to music and making bad jokes.

177: WEATHERING THE STORM

by Toni G.

It's always dark before the dawn. Change had come, just as predicted by the scientific community 50 years ago. The world was overpopulated. Resources were scarce. Food production was almost at a standstill. It was sink or swim time.

The world was now reaping what it had sown. This was the first solution to the problem of overpopulation in its most basic form: suicide. People threw themselves from roof tops, leapt out of windows and jumped in front of trains. No one knew what was driving this craze or who would be affected next.

Nonbelievers and believers alike could be found hiding in churches, praying to God or a higher power for answers. Others crowded into hospitals, begging anyone in a white lab-coat for help. Through the chaos, I held high hopes for mankind's survival. Through the chaos, I looked for a brighter tomorrow.

~

Toni G.'s Biography

Toni G. writes poetry and micro flash. More of her work may be found at The Drabble, Elephants Never and also right here @ ChristopherFielden.com (Nonsense and 81 Word Challenges).

178: OUR BRUMMIE KID'S BIRTHDAY

by Betty Hattersley

It's our kid's birthday today. He's as old as my tongue and a little bit older than my teeth. A right long thing and a thank you and as thick as two short planks most of the time.

But today he's in his best bib and tucker and as proud as a dog with two tails. We are having a trip up the cut in a canal boat. We are going to be two dirty stop outs.

Might have a beer or two later, but if he has too much to drink for two pins he'd give you a fourpenny one.

So I think we'll keep it short and sweet before he gets all over the shop.

~

Betty Hattersley's Biography

I've been writing for a few years and have had numerous poems and short stories published in anthologies, newspapers, calendars and magazines. I do enjoy these challenges.

179: GOOD OLE BOYS

by N.B. Craven

"Well, Jimmy, it's gonna be another hot one."

"Can say that again, Bubba. It's hot as Hades out here."

"Knees acting up, though. It'll be raining cats and dogs by noon."

"Heard ole Joe's boy finished digging that ditch, round the bend there."

"Yep, that boy is strong as an ox. Must be all that steak and taters they feed him."

"Don't let him hear ya say he's an ox, he'd be mad as a wet hen."

"Speaking of angry hens, you hear Tommy's daughter failed her drivin' test?"

"Nope. Guess the cat's out of the bag now, though. What happened?"

"Well, she was more worried about fixin' her pretty blonde mop than fixin' her eyes on the road."

"I'll bet she'll be cold as a witch's tit for the next couple weeks."

"Best avoid her like the plague."

"Yeah. If we don't, we might be dead as a doornail."

~

N.B. Craven's Biography

N.B. Craven is the father of four wonderful children and has been married to the most wonderful woman for 12 years. He is a southern boy at heart but has lived all over the USA. He currently resides in Tri-cities, Washington.

180: A MISUNDERSTANDING

by Klaus Gehling

After writing my memoirs, I was relaxing in a street café at the market place. I felt optimistic while sipping my latte macchiato. The sun was warming my skin and my heart.

At noon, a young man appeared punctually (as he should) asking passers-by whether they had seen his cliché. I got goose bumps. Halloween? April fool? No, it was summer, one of those shimmering hot days, in which time seemed to stand still.

Some responses were: "No, my hat is pretty enough." A man comforted, "It will be alright."

It wasn't his day. Dark clouds appeared.

Suddenly, he spotted a man with a cliché. He ran to him.

"Can I have your cliché? I've lost mine."

The cliché was a feathered hat from Bayern. I realised: *Oh, I'm in Munich.*

The worst was yet to come.

"It's not a cliché, it's a stereotype, you fool," the man answered.

~

Klaus Gehling's Biography

68 years old. Retired as a psychologist and psychotherapist, but still working now and then. I`m keen on writing short stories, playing guitar and chess and visiting excavations.

181: ABOVE AND BEYOND

by Mark Stocker

"No, Rocky, it's too dangerous."

"Sorry, chief." Rocky Fettuccine, maverick NYPD cop, ran back into the flaming building. It was hard to see a way through, but he had to try.

Driven on by his personal demons, Rocky battled up the crumbling staircase, his impressively muscled body peppered by falling debris. *If only my cruel father, who abandoned me following the tragic and untimely death of my doting mother, could see me now*, Rocky thought. "I am not a failure, Dad," he growled.

Rocky reached the first landing and kicked a door in. Through the smoke, he could see Cindy sprawled on the floor.

"My hero," she swooned, as Rocky swept her up.

"All part of the service, ma'am," said Rocky, and threw her out of the window. "Hope they got that safety net ready," he chuckled, as bricks from the collapsing walls bounced off his glistening head.

~

Mark Stocker's Biography

Mark Stocker is an advertising creative from Suffolk who loves a good cliché. He can occasionally be found online at @MarkStocker72.

182: SARAH

by Jayne Morgan

Once upon a time, Sarah was the love of my life. From the moment I saw her, I was head over heels in love. I loved her more than life itself. But, in the blink of an eye, she was gone and oh, how I missed her.

The day we met, it was love at first sight. I made it my mission to take her under my wing and bring joy, not sadness, into her life. She's only been gone a day but without her, my own life is emptier.

Sarah, however, is living the dream and doesn't have a care in the world. They say good things come to those who wait. Only time will tell, but I'm certain she will achieve great things. I may be sad but I am also immensely proud. Sarah, my baby, my little girl, is now an undergraduate at Oxford.

~

Jayne Morgan's Biography

My book *Haunted School* was published in 2005 as part of Hodder's Livewire series. Since then, I have written two more (as yet unpublished) books. When I'm not writing, I work as a support assistant to students with learning difficulties.

183: NICE GUY

by Carla Vlad

He knocked on my door and I chose to answer because I didn't want him to send me a thousand messages over night.

"Maria, you won't believe what just happened to me."

"What?"

"I met this girl and, against all the odds, she said yes to get coffee with me."

"Oh, that's—"

"They said I should follow my heart, but it's easier said than done. Maria, when she arrived, I was on cloud nine. She looked like a million bucks."

"OK…"

"I felt like a kid in a candy store. I wanted to make her mine with every fibre of my being. I asked her, 'Do you want to be my wife?' I swear, I meant to say girlfriend."

"Wow."

"I know. I started crying like a baby. I ruined my chances. She just left me. I guess good things don't come for those who wait."

"Daniel…"

~

Carla Vlad's Biography

Carla is a creative writing student with a huge passion for people and art. She is always looking for the next opportunity to learn. Someone told her she could win a Pulitzer and that is all she can think about.

184: THE MYSTERIOUS BOY

by Roberta Scafidi

"I can't love you," the mysterious boy with perfect hair told the stubborn yet sensitive girl.

"Why not?" she asked, perplexed.

"I have a dark past. I'm evil. I'm toxic." He looked out into the distance.

"Meth is toxic but I still do it."

"What?"

"I don't care about your past. We all have our demons."

"But my parents died when I was little."

"So did everyone else's."

"I have duties. I gotta save the world."

"From what?"

"From evil."

"I thought you were evil?"

"It's, uh, complicated."

"Do tell. Just because I'm a cheerleader doesn't mean I'm dumb."

"I never said you were."

"Because you're different…"

"We still can't be together."

"Why not?"

"Because… End credits."

"Did you just say 'end credits'?"

"Seemed fitting."

"So?"

"Look, I have killed."

"Boo-hoo. Anything else?"

"N-no?"

"I'm OK with that. But I gotta warn you, everyone

around me kicks the bucket."
"Oh."

~

Roberta Scafidi's Biography

Roberta Scafidi is an italian author born in Patti (Sicily) in October 1999. She's attended Classical Lyceum in her hometown and is currently studying Foreign Languages and Literature in the University of Messina.

185: TIME TO FACE THE MUSIC

by Matthew Bines

Once upon a time, in a land far, far away, an unlikely band of heroes walked into a bar. A wise wizard, a bulky dwarf, a beautiful elf and a reluctant hero teenager, who was as fit as a fiddle, postponed their quest to lick their wounds.

Behind wrinkles that were as old as the hills, the wizard said, "Take a seat everyone, today is our day off."

"It's about time. This journey has lasted an eternity," sighed the dwarf.

They sat together, ordering a round of drinks, and rested deep in thought about the dark lord's intentions.

"They say that evil never sleeps," muttered the elf.

"Quiet, elf," snapped the dwarf.

"He is right though," said the hero. "He's going to destroy the world by tomorrow. What are we to do?"

The wizard jumped from his seat, storming out of the bar. "We must face the music."

~

Matthew Bines' Biography

I am an 18-year-old aspiring writer who has had a passion for creative writing since I first picked up a book. Sci-Fi is my usual genre but I like to write anything.

186: STEREOTYPICAL SLASHER STORY

by Olivia Ackers

Lightning crackled outside; the rolling thunder boomed in the forest that surrounded us.

We sat against the wall, holding our breath as the steady footsteps closed in on us...

A floorboard creaked. Our heads turned towards the door, praying it wasn't him. My heart pounded, a rat scurried at our feet and Sam screamed at the top of her lungs as the door burst open.

A large man trudged in. His muscular arm grabbed Sam by the throat and threw her aside. I darted past him, my life flashing before my eyes, and flew down the stairs, tripping at the bottom and tumbling to the floor. I quickly recovered and fumbled with the keys to unlock the door, but before I could escape a hand clasped around my throat. As a knife impaled my back, everything faded to black...

I jolted up in bed, realising it was all a dream...

~

Olivia Ackers' Biography

My name is Olivia Ackers, I'm 17 years old and I'm a literature fanatic. I aspire to become a writer and hopefully, this will be a stepping stone towards my life dream.

187: DOUSED DREAMS

by Ibukun Keyamo

"Make hay while the sun shines," they said
   "Don't leave it too long," they said.
   And I listened to them.
   That's the part that gets me.
   I listened to them.
   Now, I have five children, aged nine months through seven years and a husband I barely see. This wasn't how my life was supposed to go. After moving to LA, my acting career was supposed to kick-off. I was supposed to have won one or two awards; maybe an Oscar before a modelling agency snatched me up and I started walking catwalks all over the world and then, one day, I would end up in Paris for a shoot and I would meet a handsome, rich, French artist and we would live happily ever after. Just thinking about Pierre (my imaginary French lover) almost made me forget reality.
   Almost.
   Until I was doused in ice water.
   Courtesy of my son.

~

Ibukun Keyamo's Biography

My name is Ibukun Keyamo. I'm a 16 year old university freshman from Nigeria. I absolutely love writing and you can almost always find me lost in a good book.

188: LADIES' DOUBLES

by Steve Lodge

Well, it just wasn't cricket, was it? We were at Foulbreath Park for the semi-finals of the cherished Dallimerski Lawn Tennis Cup to see our local heroes, the Wisby sisters, Charlene and Shirin, in ladies' doubles action against the seemingly ordinary pairing of Petunia Muncher and Honey O'Brian, both of Gravestutter in Hampshire. Winners take a place in the coveted grand final.

At the end of the day, Petunia and Honey deserved their win. To be honest, Charlene and Shirin slept through the match, basically without raising the female equivalent of a sweat, or our hopes. You know what I mean?

When I interviewed the sisters after the match, I was like, "What happened?" and they were like, "What just happened?" and they were like, "OK, we go again next match, bring it on, we'll totally nail it, we are a bottomless pit."

Gerald Reporter, *Essex Coastal Independent Echo*

~

Steve Lodge's Biography

Steve Lodge is a wandering minstrel from London now based in Singapore. He has written a number of published short stories, plays, skits, poems and lyrics. He acts and is a regular on the Singapore Improv and Stand-up comedy circuit. @steveweave71

189: TIME FLIES WHEN THE SQUEAKY WHEEL GETS THE GREASE

by Mark J Towers

"Run it by me again... why send a car into space?" Kelly asked. She thought her boss was yanking her chain.

"Have you heard the expression 'hitch your wagon to a star'?" Steve asked. "Well, this is just the tip of the iceberg. Space is the final frontier, the stuff that dreams are made of." Steve kicked the tyres for good measure. This type of project only came along once in a blue moon.

"You're living on another planet."

"Well, they do say men are from Mars, women are from Venus."

"So, what's my job?"

"You're my ace in the hole, Kelly. You know everything under the sun about this car, so you'll be the pilot. Drive at the speed of light in orbit, and come back down to earth with a bump."

Kelly wasn't exactly over the moon. In fact, this really drove her up the wall.

~

Mark J Towers' Biography

Mark J Towers writes children's books, short stories, flash fiction and poetry whenever he has spare time from 'Dad taxi' duties.

190: CRYSTAL

by Jasmine Lee

I reached to push my glasses up and began to gather all my notes and textbooks.

"I'm really sorry."

I looked up to see Chase, dressed in his football uniform. "No, it's fine. It's fine," I stuttered, accidentally brushing my fingers against his while we both tried to pick up the same book.

He ran his free hand through his hair. "Crystal, right? Don't we have chemistry together?"

"Chem-chemistry?" I asked, feeling my face redden like a tomato.

"Yeah, chem class. Second period," he responded, brushing off his letterman jacket.

BEEP, BEEP, BEEP.

"Crystal. CRYSTAL."

I soon woke up to see my mum standing over me. She quickly wrapped her arms around me. "Thank goodness you finally woke up from your coma."

"Coma?" I asked.

"Yes, you were in a really bad car crash," my mum stated.

"So, it was all a dream?"

~

Jasmine Lee's Biography

Jasmine likes to sometimes write shorts and she hopes that you somewhat enjoy her horribly, horribly clichéd story.

191: BARROOM BRAWL

by Susi J Smith

He strolled into the bar, cool as a cucumber, a real smooth operator, and sauntered up to me.

"Name your poison."

I couldn't blame him for trying; I'm cute as a button and was dressed to kill. But he was all sizzle, no steak and barking up the wrong tree. "Take a hike."

He shrugged. "Bottoms up." He drank like a fish and was soon drunk as a skunk. "I won't beat around the bush, you're as ugly as sin but beggars can't be choosers so let's blow this joint."

I threw up my hands in disgust. "Read my lips, you're playing with fire. Don't push your luck."

"Well, feast your eyes on this." He darted to and fro, dancing with two left feet. "So? How do you like them apples?"

This was the last straw. I decided to drive the point home and bury the hatchet... in his head.

~

Susi J Smith's Biography

Susi J Smith adores alliteration and word play, particularly puns. She enjoys writing short stories, and flash fiction. Susi lives in Scotland where she longs for a writing room of her own.

192: THE LAST PLAGUE

by Majella Pinto

When life gives you lemons, make lemonade. A quarantined family that watches livestreaming mass on Facebook together stays together in order to save bandwidth. Stocked up for Armageddon, I find a lot of spare time on my hands.

"You are lucky," says my friend, over the phone, who made two trips to Costco but didn't find toilet paper.

"Three times is a charm," I tell her and, lo and behold, she followed the instructions to the T this time and was there when the doors opened.

She's as slow as a turtle, so, when she reached the aisle, she was lucky to get the last two rolls. Everything that glitters is not gold, but this was more valuable than the free diamond ring that was on the meme being circulated along with a picture of a toilet roll with a purple bow on it. She felt like a lucky dog.

~

Majella Pinto's Biography

Majella Pinto, raised in India, is an artist and writer based in California. She works in Silicon Valley and is devoutly focused on her twin passions of art and literature.

www.facebook.com/majella.pinto

193: THE GREAT BLUNDER

by Ashutosh Pant

I'm really amazed how people who are so famous and so respected can lose their reputation in a matter of minutes.

I am a scientist and, as actions speak louder than words, was respected for discovering that the fourth dimension was time. But now, as an action of a split second, I am here hiding from those same people who respected me.

As haste makes waste, I made a blunder by mixing the wrong chemicals, almost creating an artificial sun. It could have destroyed the Earth, but actions speak louder than words and Eva was there. She managed to prevent it.

Somehow, the news went viral at the speed of light and I'm here hiding.

~

Ashutosh Pant's Biography

My name is Ashutosh Pant from Kathmandu, Nepal. I study in class 7, Alok Vidyashram. I am 13 years old.

194: A RAT IN THE ALAMO

by Benjamin Noel

"Hey, Simmons, whadaya think about the new kid on patrol?"

"Who? Henry, the kid from Queens?"

"Yea, him. Top brass scraped the bottom of the barrel with this new guy."

"Guess he's a little strange. Whadaya sayin'? He don't bat straight or what?"

"No, no, not that, it's—"

"Well, whadaya saying? Shoot it to me straight. C'mon, give me something to bite on here."

"Well, here, don't you smell something fishy? He's been asking Winters all these questions; how we run the scam. Even a rookie knows, when it gets dirty, the right hand don't know and sure don't bother with what the left's doing. Kid stinks to high heaven."

"Woa there, cowboy. You saying the kid's a bad apple? We got a rat in—"

"Hey, hey, keep it down."

"He'll rat out the whole bunch. God knows who he's flipped."

"He's gonna get what's coming."

~

Benjamin Noel's Biography

Hailing from the San Francisco bay area, I, Benjamin, enjoy watching films and reading books. And after being voluntold to try this challenge by my mum and my grandma, have decided to begin writing creatively, and find myself here.

195: PLAYING THE FIELD

by Roger Woodcock

Billy always said I were a wet blanket. "There was never a dull moment with Elsie," he use to ram down my throat. I found the lass dull as ditchwater but then I would, wouldn't I, Elsie being his mistress.

I use to think he were pure as the driven snow, Billy. "Play your cards right and I'm all yours," he use to say. Mam sussed him out, said an apple never falls far from the tree. But there's none so blind as them what can't see. I was like a kid in a candy store until I found out Mam was right.

Elsie's gone now. I could see beauty was only skin deep when I looked down on her razored face. Me, I don't put all my eggs in one basket no more. Play the field. That's what I'm doing now.

~

Roger Woodcock's Biography

Came to serious writing after retirement from BT. Have had several short stories published in obscure magazines but after turning my hand to playwriting had mind-numbing success after my play *Darra's Coffin* was performed in Swindon and Australia.

196: A PERFECT STORM

by Jude Higgins

After he complained the chips were burned, her eyes brimmed with tears that splashed into the salt pot on the table between them. He put the pot in the sun to dry.

"You ruin everything," he said. "First the chips, then the salt."

"So make the chips yourself next time," she said. "Salt is bad for you anyway."

His face was livid, like storm clouds.

"Men like me are the salt of the earth," he said, dousing his chips with vinegar.

She smiled, faintly. "Women like me are worth their weight in gold."

He relaxed. "Perhaps I'm making a storm in a teacup," he said, hugging her. "The chips are OK really. Cheer up, my treasure. Worse things happen at sea."

She hugged him back, wondering if, given the latest news, that view still held water.

"No shortage of salt out there anyway," she joked.

~

Jude Higgins' Biography

Jude Higgins is a writer of short fiction, published widely in magazines and anthologies. Her chapbook *The Chemist's House* was published by V. Press in 2017. She organises Bath Flash Fiction Award and directs Flash Fiction Festivals, UK.

www.judehiggins.com

197: THE ULTIMATE SOLUTION

by John Lane

Once upon a time in a galaxy far, far away, there lived a man whose marriage seemed to last an eternity because his wife nagged like there was no tomorrow.

Whenever he drove his taxi at the speed of light throughout his home planet and lost track of time regarding his need to be at his wife's side, it was only a matter of time before his spouse blew a gasket.

She always sang the same old tune. "If I've said it once, I've said it a million times, get home early to help out with the housework because I'm not your personal maid. But it goes in one ear and out the other. All I do is talk until I'm blue in the face."

So, he did what his wife always wanted.

He got divorced and hired a personal maid.

~

John Lane's Biography

John Lane has work published at 81words.net, Flash Fiction North, Carrot Ranch Literary Community, Fifty Word Stories, The Drabble, Trembling With Fear and elsewhere. Currently a volunteer editor for 101 Words. Army and National Guard Veteran.

198: STARTING SIGNAL

by Annika Franke

A journey of a thousand miles begins with a single step, I try to convince myself, but I'm a bundle of nerves. This is because I have a memory like an elephant. I will always remember the insults saying I'm a freak, I'm out of my mind and I have a screw loose.

However, I know I could give all my blood, sweat and tears for this project. From day one, I could put my heart and soul into it. The sky would be the limit. And yet, I'm still waiting for the right moment to come. Should I try? Should I take the risk?

Someone taps on my back, scaring me to death. With a deep voice, he declares, "Actions speak louder than words."

~

Annika Franke's Biography

Annika Franke enjoys travelling with floating islands, talking to dragons and using magical hourglasses. No, she isn't crazy (and she should know it because she studies psychology), she just loves writing.

199: ALL'S FAIR IN LOVE AND WAR

by DT Langdale

Rex Stone stared at a fate far worse than death. Her name was Cynthia. He wanted to calm her down, to make her see sense and lower the gun. But he couldn't dislodge the frog in his throat. Water splashed against the pier. The moon sparkled in her sequins.

"You've got some nerve, Rex." Her voice was silky smooth. "Always showing up, like a bad penny."

"Call it a habit."

"How'd you know I stole it?"

"Your perfume." He lit a cigarette, blew the smoke skyward. "The diamond case smelt like my pillow."

A smile played at the corner of Cynthia's lips. "Come with me."

For a split second, Rex glimpsed their future: fencing a stolen diamond, bouncing from country to country, always on the run. She dropped the gun, leant in, kissed him.

"What time's the ferry?" he asked.

Hell, all's fair in love and war. Right?

~

DT Langdale's Biography

Dave is a professional copywriter and newly published author. When not writing, he's often found in a pub or near cats. Or writing in a pub that has cats.

www.davelangdale.com

200: THE AVENGER

by Matilda Pinto

A long time ago, on a dark and stormy night, Ms Geralyn warbled, "Favourable weather for a ghost story, no?"

"Not again," whispered the threesome.

Though drunk like fish, they could never forget that bike ride and the ravishing beauty they had stumbled into at Kadri market. Seated on a rickety chair, dressed in white, hair let loose, she kept rocking back and forth. With josh they had whistled and cackled to miff her, to no avail.

Speeding past Bendore cemetery, Ponnu had challenged Ravi to jump over the wall and kiss the grave of a dead. Having jumped, he buckled. So, did they. For, in the pitch-dark night, they had seen the same beauty in white, seated on a grave, rocking. Shuddering, they had hauled Ravi over the wall and scooted from there.

For the next couple of days, every fibre of Ravi's being was beset, and theirs, harried.

~

Matilda Pinto's Biography

Matilda is for real; a living, breathing creature. She validates her existence with her writing, a novel titled *Fisticuffs of the Soul* and a few short stories. Besides, she holds a passport and membership to organisations such as the Toastmasters.

www.facebook.com/matilda.pinto.9

TRITELY CHALLENGED

A FINAL NOTE

Jude and I would like to say one last THANK YOU to all the authors featured in this anthology. Their generosity is helping support a very worthy charity and it's an honour to present their stories in this collection.

Don't forget to check my website for more writing challenges. You will be able to find all the details here: www.christopherfielden.com/writing-challenges/

There is also an 'Authors of the Flash Fiction Writing Challenges' Facebook group that runs its own regular challenges. It's open to everyone. Please feel free to join here:
www.facebook.com/groups/157928995061095/

I bid you farewell Bristol-style:

Cheers me dears,

Chris Fielden

Printed in Great Britain
by Amazon